This book belongs to

_____

The Western Frostings

Sugarplum
Mines

The
Lak

Zuckerbrote
Peak

Donkey's Causeway

The

Rocks

Drosselmeyer P

Dro

The

Rocky
Falls

King
Caspar's
Mines

Rushing River

vs

Leopard's
Paradise

The City The

Forest

eyer Plains

alley

R. Verbena

Toffee-Apple
Orchards

The Eastern Frosting

Crystal Coldwater

Emerald Everhart

Illustrated by
Patricia Ann Lewis-MacDougall

EGMONT

EGMONT

We bring stories to life

Crystal Coldwater first published in 2008
by Egmont UK Limited
239 Kensington High Street
London W8 6SA

Text copyright © 2008 Angela Woolfe
Illustrations copyright © 2008 Patricia Ann Lewis-MacDougall

The moral rights of the author and illustrator have been asserted

ISBN 978 1 4052 3327 9

1 3 5 7 9 10 8 6 4 2

A CIP catalogue record for this title is available from the British Library

Printed and bound in Italy by L.E.G.O. S.P.A

Contents

Prologue

When I was a young Ballerina, an admirer gave me a gift.

It was only a frosted-glass perfume bottle, filled with a sweet scent of lemon and orange. But my admirer told me that

the bottle was the most precious thing he could give, because there was a magical Kingdom inside.

I didn't believe him at first.

But that night, I had a very special dream. I dreamed of a magical Kingdom, the most beautiful land I'd ever seen, filled with delightful people and their very special animals. And the next time I danced, I thought of the Kingdom, and suddenly I danced as I had never danced before. Every night that I wore the perfume, I danced

better than ever, until I was the most
famous Ballerina in the world.

But one day, the old frosted-glass bottle
was accidentally thrown away.

And from that day onwards, I never
danced so beautifully again.

I searched for the bottle high and low,
but I never found it. I have since had many
years to write down what I learned about
the Kingdom inside . . .

Inside the bottle, behind snow-capped
Frosty Mountains, the Kingdom is divided

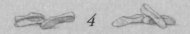

4

into five parts. There are frozen Lakes in the north, warmer meadows in the southern Valley, stark grey Rocks in the west, and to the east, a deep, dark Forest.

And the City. How could I forget the City? Silverberg, the capital, rising from the

Drosselmeyer Plains like a beautiful new jewel on an old ring.

From a distance, the houses seem to be piled on top of each other. Their brightly painted wooden roofs look as if they hold up the floors of the dwellings above as they wind around and around ever-more-narrow streets. And at the very top of the teetering pile is the biggest building of all: the Royal Palace. It is made from snow-white marble taken from the Frosty Mountains themselves, which glows in the *early morning sun and sparkles in the cold night.*

The Royal Palace is the home of the King and Queen. But it is here too, within

the marble walls of the Palace, that you can find the Kingdom's famous Royal Ballet School. This is where the most talented young Ballerinas in the land become proper Ballerinas-in-Training, and really learn to dance. They travel from far and wide. Pale blonde Lake girls journey from the north, dark-haired Valley Dwellers come from the south. Grey-eyed Ballerinas travel from the western Rocks, and green-eyed Forest girls make their way from the east. The City girls have no need to come quite so far.

Of course, they all bring their pets. Each Kingdom Dweller has their own animal companion. And these animals can talk — talk just like you and me. Lake Dwellers keep Arctic foxes or snow leopards, while Valley Dwellers keep small tigers, monkeys or exotic birds. Strong, sturdy Rock Dwellers enjoy the company of sheep, goats and donkeys, while Forest Dwellers keep black bears and leopards. Every City Dweller keeps an eagle.

Out there, somewhere, is my old

frosted-glass perfume bottle.

Out there, somewhere, are the Ballerinas-in-Training who inspired me — Jessica Juniper, Crystal Coldwater, Laura-Bella Bergamotta, Valentina de la Frou and Ursula of the Boughs.

And they will wait for you, until the day that you find them.

Emerald Everhart

CHAPTER ONE
The Project

A new term at the Royal Ballet School had begun. The New Year's air was fresh with possibility, and Jessica Juniper and her four best friends were determined to work harder than ever.

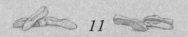

'My New Year's resolution is to get better marks in Mime,' said Jessica, over the breakfast table.

'My New Year's resolution is to do more Ballet practice,' sighed Crys, the

Lake Dweller, although she was already the best dancer in the class.

'I suppose I should try harder at Costume, Hair and Make-up,' laughed Laura-Bella, the Valley Dweller.

'I promised Dad I'd learn a new musical instrument,' said Ursula, in her low voice. 'Forest Dwellers are supposed to play two or three instruments at least.'

'And I'm going to write the best History of Ballet project ever,' said Valentina, tossing her long, long blonde hair. 'Master Silas thinks I'm just a silly, spoilt City Dweller, but I'm going to show him I'm smart, too. Project Day, here I come!'

They were all excited about Project

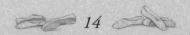

Day tomorrow. There would be no ordinary lessons. Instead, the girls would form into groups and spend all day working on their projects in the library. The best group project would win each girl a star, and a trip to the Grand Tea-Rooms in town for delicious toasted Flumpets and Caramel-crunch Cupcakes.

'I hope Master Silas chooses a good topic. Last year's Beginners had to do a project about the building of the Palace Theatre,' sighed Laura-Bella. 'Boring!'

'But the year before that was even worse.' Jessica had quizzed a third-year pupil about this. 'Their project was all about the history of the flugelhorn and the pifflepipe.'

'Well, let's hope this year it's about the history of the hair ribbon and the powder puff,' teased Crys, nudging Valentina. 'That way, our team is bound to do well, isn't it, Val?'

'My New Year's resolution,' came the loud voice of Jessica's pet donkey, Sinbad,

'is to eat nothing but Raspberry Flancakes.' He shook his long ears happily. 'You may ask, why particularly Raspberry Flancakes. Why not Cinnamon Twists and Iced Passion-Fruit Tarts? Well . . .'

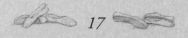

'I can assure you, Mr Donkey, that we shall be asking nothing of the sort!' Laura-Bella's tiger, Mr Melchior, frowned. But Ursula's pet bear, Dorothea, and Valentina's eagle, Olympia, gave oohs and ahhs, impressed by Sinbad's New Year's resolution. Only Pollux, Crys's white fox, made no comment. As usual, he stayed quiet and simply blinked his wise, gentle eyes.

Everyone in the Beginners' class was excited about the project announcement.

Even Rubellina Goodfellow, the Chancellor's daughter, forgot to whisper nasty things about Jessica and her friends as they all took their seats in Master Silas's classroom. Rubellina was too busy showing off her new pink sequinned pencil case, stuffed with golden ink-pens and scented erasers.

'Daddy gave it to me,' she boasted to her friend Jo-Jo. 'He told me I was bound to win on Project Day anyway, but this will help.'

Jessica and Crys rolled their eyes at each other.

'Rubellina will win – if the project is about Horrible Chancellors' Daughters,' whispered Jessica.

'Horrible Chancellors' Daughters With Brand New Pencil Cases!' Crys said back, slightly too loudly. She got a spiteful glare from Rubellina for her trouble.

'Good morning, girls,' said Master Silas, entering the classroom in a swirl of blue velvet, and giving them a rare, sudden smile. 'You are all on time this morning, for a change! Even you goats at the back.'

Master Silas was not being rude. There really was a group of goats at the back. They were all sitting down comfortably beside Sinbad the donkey. Usually, pets did not attend classes. Even the City Dwellers' eagles, who could simply have sat quietly on their owners' shoulders and dropped off to sleep,

usually spent lesson times gossiping in the cosy dormitory. Sinbad, however, came to every single class, except the ones he had been banned from. Now several of the Rock Dwellers' goats, who all adored Sinbad, had started to come to class, too.

'And me, Master Silas!' Sinbad waggled his long ears. 'Don't forget me!'

'Forgetting you, Sinbad, is impossible,' said Master Silas, with a twitch of his eyebrow. 'Now, girls, turn to page fifty-two in your Nutcracker Ballet textbooks . . .'

The lesson was long and not very interesting. Even Jessica, who adored History of Ballet classes, fidgeted and sighed her way through the session, desperate to hear what the project would be. Precisely two minutes before the end-of-class bell rang up in the Clock Tower, Master Silas closed his own textbook with a thud, and limped around to stand in front of his desk.

'I can tell by your excitement that none of you has forgotten about Project Day. I've never seen a group of dancers so eager to be given homework!'

No one giggled at his joke. They were too impatient to find out what their project would be about.

Master Silas smiled. 'Well, girls, I won't keep you waiting. This is the subject for Project Day.' He turned to the blackboard behind him, picked up his usual piece of pale blue chalk, and wrote seven words in his looping handwriting.

The Life and Work of Eva Snowdrop

Jessica forgot how strict Master Silas was, and clapped her hands in delight. Fortunately everyone else in the class was doing the same.

Eva Snowdrop!

Eva Snowdrop was everybody's favourite dancer, the most famous Prima Ballerina the Kingdom had ever known.

The girls all had pictures of her pinned up in their lockers and above their beds, in the hope that a tiny part of Eva Snowdrop's talent would rub off on them. But she had not been Prima Ballerina for very long. Twenty years ago, she had fallen in love with a man known only as the Mystery Lake Fisherman. She left the Royal Ballet behind, to live with him up in the northern Lakes. The beautiful Prima Ballerina with the whole Kingdom at her perfect feet gave up dancing for love. She had never been seen in Silverberg again.

'Your projects must be handed in at the end of the day tomorrow,' Master

Silas said, smiling at their excitement. 'There will be no normal lessons, but you must all spend the day working hard!'

Laura-Bella grabbed Jessica's hand. 'Aren't we lucky, Jessica? Eva Snowdrop is my favourite ballerina ever! This is so much better than writing about silly old flugelhorns or pifflepipes.'

Jessica turned to Crys, who was still sitting at her desk. 'Eva Snowdrop!' Jessica began. 'Isn't it brilliant . . .'

Then she stopped.

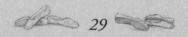

Crys's face was the colour the sky turns when it is about to snow. She looked as if she might be sick.

'Crys, are you all right?' Jessica hurried towards her, but Crys sprang to her feet.

'Fine,' she said. Her voice was trembling. 'I'm fine.'

And, almost knocking her friends over in her haste, Crys ran from the classroom.

CHAPTER TWO
Crys's Secret

Jessica, Laura-Bella, Valentina and Ursula skipped lunch to look for Crys. Helped by their pets – although Sinbad's panic was rather unhelpful – they searched the school from top to bottom, trying to find their friend.

Crys was not in the dormitory, nor in any of the ballet practice rooms. She was not in the Winter Garden, where they sometimes had tea in the afternoons, nor was she in the Beginners' Common Room.

'Looking for something, Jessie?' Rubellina Goodfellow asked, sugary-sweet. She was sitting with Jo-Jo and their eagles in the Common Room's most comfortable chairs. 'Can I help at all?'

'No, thank you, Rubellina,' said Jessica.

'Because me and Jo-Jo were just wondering if you were searching for a bar of soap.' Rubellina wrinkled her delicate nose. 'It smells like it's an awfully long time since you used any.'

She and Jo-Jo burst into high-pitched giggles.

'Ignore her,' said Ursula, in her quiet voice, as Jessica went red. 'When I had to be her friend, she said that kind of thing about everyone behind their backs.'

Jessica just wished that Rubellina would stop saying that kind of thing to her face.

Worried by Crys's disappearance, the four friends were relieved to see her when they hurried along to the afternoon Mime class. Crys was already in the Mime studio, wearing the black Mime leotard all the girls hated. She was warming up at the barre, and her white fox Pollux was dozing peacefully around her neck.

'Crys!' Laura-Bella cried when she saw her. 'Where have you been?'

'Here and there,' said Crys, with a shrug.

'Well, you might have been here rather than there!' Angry now that she was no longer worried, Valentina stamped her foot. 'We've been searching all over for you!'

Jessica could see that Crys's eyes were puffy, as though she had been crying. Crys never cried. 'Crys, what's wrong?' Jessica asked.

'Nothing.' Crys turned away. 'Please, you four, leave me alone.'

'Well!' Valentina tossed her hair.

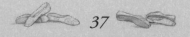

Sinbad copied her, flinging his ears about and letting out a bad-tempered bray. 'That's nice,' huffed Valentina. 'That's what I call manners.'

Crys looked as if she might burst into tears again as Valentina and Sinbad stamped off to another corner of the Mime studio.

'Val was just worried,' explained Laura-Bella, trying to pat Crys's arm.

'We're just glad you didn't disappear altogether!' said Jessica, trying to make a joke. She was glad when Crys rewarded her with a watery smile.

Valentina appeared to have forgotten her anger by supper-time, and the five friends sat together with their pets at their usual table. They tucked into slices of delicious Pumpkin-and-Potato Pie and gravy, with Snowberry Crumble for afters. Sinbad refused any pie, and munched instead at the Raspberry Flancakes he'd persuaded Cook to make for him.

'OK, gang, can we start our project now?' Sinbad asked, after nine huge Flancakes. He'd started to feel rather sick, and wanted an excuse to stop eating. 'Eva Snowdrop's my favourite ballerina, and I've got all kinds of stories to write about her . . .'

Crys suddenly seemed to choke on her Crumble. For a moment, it looked as if she would burst into tears. Then, before anyone could say a word, she put down her spoon, picked Pollux up from the seat beside her and wrapped him around her neck.

'Everyone, follow me,' she said, getting to her feet.

Exchanging worried glances, the others followed.

With her head held very high, Crys hurried them out of the Hall, across the Winter Garden, and towards the Old Library.

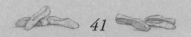

'It will be quiet in here,' she said, pushing open the tall, golden door. She was right. As most of the Ballerinas-in-Training were finishing up their supper, the Old Library was almost empty. Only one or two girls and their pets were dotted around the huge room, browsing among the tall bookshelves or curled up reading on the velvet sofas.

The friends followed Crys to the darkest, quietest corner she could find. When they were all huddled around,

Pollux opened his eyes. Their bright blue glow lit up the darkness, so that everyone could see.

'I'm going to tell you a secret,' whispered Crys. 'But you have to promise you won't tell a soul.'

'Of course we won't!' Jessica began, but Crys held up a hand.

'You have to swear,' she said. 'Lake Dwellers' Vow.'

Jessica, Laura-Bella, Valentina and Ursula put their hands on top of Crys's.

'You pets must swear too,' said Crys. 'I know you don't have hands, but you must all look into Pollux's eyes and swear you

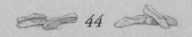

won't tell anyone. Especially you, Sinbad.'

Sinbad gave an outraged harrumph.

'Sinbad's good at keeping secrets,' Jessica promised. 'Honestly he is.'

Crys clasped her friends' hands tightly. 'I swear not to tell . . .'

'I swear not to tell,' repeated the other four.

'. . . a single, solitary soul . . .' said Crys.

'. . . a single, solitary soul . . .' they all said.

'. . . what Crystal Coldwater, Lake Dweller, is about to tell me,' Crys finished.

Now Jessica knew it was really serious. Crys never used her full name.

'. . . what Crystal Coldwater, Lake Dweller, is about to tell me,' the other four echoed.

Crys stared around at them all in the strange blue light from Pollux's eyes.

'Eva Snowdrop,' she whispered, 'is my mother.'

CHAPTER THREE
Promises

The four other girls stared at Crys.

'What do you mean?' Jessica managed to ask.

'Just what I say.' Crys's face was flushed. 'My mum was – is – Eva

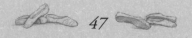

Snowdrop. Well, her name's Eva Coldwater now, because she married my dad.'

'Your dad is the Mystery Lake Fisherman?' Valentina gasped.

Crys shrugged. 'Yes. But to me, he's just . . . well . . . Dad.'

There was silence for a moment, broken, as usual, by Sinbad.

'Wow!' the donkey said.

'Crys, why didn't you tell us before?' Laura-Bella squeaked. 'This is amazing!'

'This is why I didn't tell you before!' Crys pointed a shaking finger around at her friends. 'All this fuss! You'll all treat me differently now. You'll all think I ought to be a better dancer, and you'll only want to know me because of Mum, not because you really like me . . .'

'That's just not true!' Jessica cried. 'We all love Eva Snowdrop, but you're our friend, Crys. We won't think of you differently at all!'

'And you're already the best dancer in

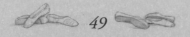

the class,' said Ursula, peering out from beneath her long fringe. 'If you got any better, you'd just be . . .'

'Scary,' filled in Laura-Bella.

The five friends burst out laughing.

'Seriously, wow,' repeated Sinbad, his

eyes like saucers. He nudged Pollux with his long nose. 'Come on, Pol, spill the beans! What's it like living with Eva Snowdrop?'

'Sinbad, behave!' snapped Mr Melchior, Laura-Bella's tiger. 'Pollux does not blab everything to everyone, unlike some pets I could mention.'

'Spoilsport,' muttered Sinbad.

'But Crys, aren't you proud of your mum?' Valentina was finding it just as hard not to ask questions. 'I mean, she was Eva Snowdrop.'

'Of course I am!' said Crys. 'But I know what happens when you tell people. When my older sister was a pupil here a few years ago, she told someone about Mum. It was a huge mistake. Everyone started whispering in the corridors, and watching her from the back of ballet class. *Why isn't she a better dancer? . . . let's get her to invite us home for the holidays so we can meet her mum . . .'* Crys let out a long, weary sigh. 'After that, my sister only stayed for one term. She gave up her dream of being a Ballerina because she didn't want to be compared to Eva Snowdrop all the time.'

Jessica squeezed Crys's hand. 'We promise, Crys, we won't ever tell a soul. Isn't that right, everyone?'

'Yes, yes,' the others assured her. 'We promise!'

'Thank you,' said Crys, squeezing Jessica's hand back. 'I feel so much better now I've told you.'

But around the other side of the bookshelf, somebody else was listening. It was Rubellina Goodfellow, and with her was her best friend, Jo-Jo.

Now two more Beginners had a very big secret.

CHAPTER FOUR
Hot Gossip

The next morning, it only took a few minutes to realise that something unusual was happening.

Crys was making her bed neatly when she heard whispers coming from across the Beginners' dormitory. She glanced up to see Holly Millpond and Caterina Castello staring at her.

'Is something the matter?' Crys demanded.

Holly and Caterina looked rather scared of Crys's short temper, and scurried away without saying a word. Crys carried on making her bed, and folding her pink pyjamas, and put the strange moment out of her mind.

But at breakfast, something even

more peculiar happened. Every single girl in the school fell silent as Crys walked into the hall. Eighty pairs of eyes watched her as she helped herself to toast and Snowberry Jam from the big table.

'Have I got something on my skirt?' Crys asked, sitting down at her usual table with her friends. 'Everyone seems to be looking at me.'

Jessica glanced about at the Banquet Hall, startled at the faces staring in their

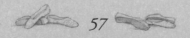

direction. 'You're right, Crys. Everyone is looking.'

Crys's ice blue eyes suddenly grew wide. 'You don't think they know, do you?'

'How could they possibly know?' Valentina scoffed. 'The only people who know about . . . well, about that thing you told us yesterday are me, Jess, Ursula and Laura-Bella. And we swore not to tell!'

'That's true.' Crys seemed comforted. 'Perhaps it's because I haven't brushed my hair yet or something.'

'I'll do your hair for you,' sighed Valentina, pulling out the comb she always kept in one of her skirt pockets. 'I wish you'd take more care about your looks, Crys. You could be just as beautiful as your mother if you tried!'

'Valentina!' gasped Jessica, worried that Crys would be upset. But Crys was smiling slightly as Valentina started to comb her hair. It looked as if sharing her deep secret with her friends had started

to make her feel better.

The others were eager to get good seats in the library for the start of Project

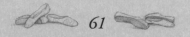 *61*

Day, so Crys hurried back to the dormitory by herself to fetch her hair ribbons. Then, excited about the day ahead, working with her friends, she skipped down the spiral stairs and towards the library. The corridor was filled with Ballerinas-in-Training, hurrying to their own lessons. But as Crys passed by, each and every one stopped and stared at her.

Their whispers were low at first, but they quickly grew faster and faster, and louder and louder. 'Is she really . . . that's what I heard . . . don't believe it . . . why not ask her . . . Eva Snowdrop . . . Eva Snowdrop . . . Eva Snowdrop . . .'

'Crys Coldwater?' A third-year girl called Binky tapped her on the shoulder. 'Is it really true, what everyone's saying?'

Crys's heart was beating very fast, but she simply gazed coolly at Binky. 'Well, that depends what everyone's saying, I suppose.'

'You know – that you're Eva

Snowdrop's daughter.'

Crys did not reply. She felt as though she might be sick. She put her head down and tried to carry on walking.

'So it is true!' shrieked Binky.

'I didn't say that!' Crys spun around.

'But you didn't deny it!' Binky grabbed Crys's arm. 'Oh, wow, Crys, this is amazing! Will you sit with me and my friends at lunch, and tell us all about her?'

'Binky, leave her alone,' said a red-haired fourth-year girl Crys did not know. 'She'll come and sit with us, won't you, Crys?'

'Crys, my dad works for the *Frosty Gazette*,' came Caterina Castello's voice now, as girls crowded around. 'You could give him an interview, all about what it's like to have Eva Snowdrop as your mum! He'll print your photo and everything.'

'Does she help you practise at home?' asked the red-haired girl.

'Does she think you're as good as she was?' asked another fourth-year.

'Do you think you're as good as she was?' asked yet another.

'Yeah, it must be really weird for you,' said Binky. 'I mean, no offence, Crys, but you'd have to be a seriously amazing dancer to ever be even half as good as Eva Snowdrop!'

The words cut into Crys like a sharp knife. 'Who told you all this?' she croaked, somehow finding her voice. 'How did you find out?'

'Your friends, of course,' said Binky.

'Those four girls you're always hanging around with. Jessica Juniper and the others. They were talking about it in the Beginners' Common Room last night, I heard, or at least . . .'

Crys did not wait to hear any more. She put her head down, and ran back up the spiral stairs.

'. . . at least, that's what Rubellina Goodfellow said,' finished Binky, gazing after Crys.

But Crys had not heard. All she

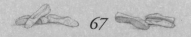

could hear as she fled towards the dormitory was Eva Snowdrop, Eva Snowdrop, Eva Snowdrop. All she heard as she pulled her small suitcase from under her bed, and started to stuff it with her clothes, was Eva Snowdrop, Eva Snowdrop, Eva Snowdrop. It was all she heard as she pulled on her light blue cloak and hat. It was all she heard as she picked her fox Pollux up from her bed and put him around her neck. And it was all she heard as she ran, tears in her eyes, for the dormitory door.

'Are we going somewhere?' asked Pollux, softly, waking up.

'Yes, Pollux! We're going far, far, far away,' Crys gulped, wishing she had a

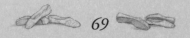

hanky. 'My friends have told everyone about Mum, so we can't stay here a moment longer!'

Pollux's eyes went wide. 'I wonder if you're more upset because everybody knows your secret,' he said, 'or because your friends betrayed you.'

'Shut up, Pollux!' said Crys, fiercely. 'If you can't say something helpful, then don't say anything at all.'

CHAPTER FIVE
North-Bound

Near Silverberg's North Gate, red-cloaked City Dwellers were busy going about their business. They were on their way to Market, or hurrying to get to work on time. So nobody paid much

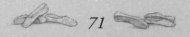

attention to the two young Ballerinas, the large brown donkey and the small, graceful eagle as they made their way towards the Gate.

'Are you sure Crys has really run away?' Valentina asked Jessica. 'Maybe she's just gone for a very long walk or something.'

'You heard what happened,' said Jessica. 'Caterina Castello just told me that Rubellina was telling everyone she heard Crys's secret from us. Crys thinks we're the ones who told everyone about her mum. Now all her things are packed and gone. She's bound to go home to the Lake, so that's where we're going.'

'We'll be in so much trouble when the teachers find out we've gone,' moaned Sinbad. 'Executed, probably.'

'It's Project Day,' said Jessica. 'No one will notice we're gone for hours. Besides, Laura-Bella and Ursula are going to tell people that we've shut ourselves away somewhere to work really hard on our Project.' She started to walk faster. 'But if we hurry, we might even get to the Lake and back again in time for tea!'

'Tea!' gasped Sinbad. 'Quick, you two, hop on my back and we'll ride there.'

'Hmmph,' said Valentina, as she and Jessica hopped on Sinbad's back, and Olympia the eagle soared above. 'You've forgotten that we have to persuade Crys to come back to school with us. And if you ask me, that'll take so long we won't

even be back for tomorrow's tea.'

Sinbad brayed and started to gallop.

Jessica hoped Valentina was wrong. Project Day or not, Laura-Bella and

Ursula could never keep the teachers from discovering that they were missing for that long.

The noise of the city faded away as they rode beyond its walls. Jessica knew that the Kingdom's sun rose in the North and set in the South, so all they had to do was follow the rising sun in a straight line. After an hour of riding, Silverberg was so far away behind them that it seemed a tiny dot in the distance. The Drosselmeyer Plains were golden in the morning light, but there was a freezing wind that pulled at the girls' cloaks and whipped Valentina's long, long hair about. Soon the ground was so icy that Sinbad started to slip and slide, and the air was so cold that his ears developed frost on the tips.

'If we hadn't been in such a hurry,' Sinbad shivered, 'I'd have put on a woolly hat instead of this fancy City hat. My ears might freeze off! How can I be a proper donkey without my ears?'

At this, Olympia the eagle let out a horrified squawk, and flew down from above to land on Sinbad's head. She sat there, warming his frozen ears, as they travelled further and further into the icy North.

Jessica almost cheered with relief when she saw the Lake come into view ahead.

'Look, everyone!' she cried. 'Isn't it beautiful?'

The Lake was ice-blue, and completely frozen. A delicate white mist

hovered all around, so that they could not see across to the other shore. There were tall pine trees beside the water's edge, and a group of timber cottages, huddled together as if for warmth. Groups of fishermen and fisherwomen sat on wooden stools on the ice, their white foxes and snow leopards wrapped around their shoulders, fishing through little holes into the water below.

'B . . . b . . . b . . . beautiful,' shivered Valentina. 'B . . . b . . . b . . . but how d . . . d . . . d . . . do we know where t . . . t . . . t . . . to find C-C-C-Crys?'

'We'll have to ask these fisher-people,' said Jessica. She cupped her hands around her mouth, ready to shout down to them on the ice, when suddenly she felt something very cold whack her right on the forehead.

'Don't shout!'

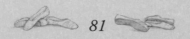

hissed the person who had just thrown a snowball at her. 'The noise might make the ice crack, and they'll all fall in. You won't be very popular then!'

It was a very tall girl, several years older than Jessica and Valentina, who had thrown the snowball. She hurried towards them, sticking her fishing rod under her arm. She was white-blonde and blue-eyed, with a rosy-cheeked, friendly face, and she had a white fox, a little bigger than Crys's, wrapped around her shoulders.

'Don't you know you have to be quiet in the Lake? Even if your shouting didn't crack the ice, you might cause an avalanche in the mountains.' The girl pointed up towards the huge, white Frosty Mountains, which Jessica and Valentina could just see through the mist. 'Well, I don't have to ask if you're from around here! My name's Sapphire, and this is my fox, Castor. Are you lost?'

'Sort of,' said Jessica. 'We've come to look for our friend, Crys Coldwater. Do you know where we might find her?'

Sapphire frowned. 'I know Crys Coldwater. Is everything all right?'

'No, it isn't all right,' announced Sinbad. 'Nasty, stinky Rubellina Goodfellow found out about her mum being Eva Snowdrop, and so Crys ran away, but we've come to find her and take her back. Hey!' he added, delightedly, watching his breath come out like white smoke in the freezing air. 'Look – I'm making fog!'

'Why she'd want to come b-b-b-back and live here instead of the lovely c-c-c-comfortable city, I d-d-d-don't know,' said Valentina, who'd had enough of her travels.

'I can take you to Crys's house,' said Sapphire. 'But it's at the most northerly tip of the Lake.'

'It would be,' groaned Valentina.

'The fastest route is straight across the Lake,' Sapphire said, with a grin. 'Do you know the best way to do that?'

They shook their heads.

'Then you're in for some fun. Follow me, everyone.' Sapphire began to walk towards the nearby row of wooden cottages. 'We're going to get some Icicle Bicycles!'

CHAPTER SIX
Across the Lake

Jessica and the others watched in amazement as the craftsman in one of the cottages made the Icicle Bicycles. Working with huge chunks of ice, his knife flew about so fast that it sent showers of ice chips raining down all around them. Very soon he had created three beautiful, glittering bicycles, made completely of ice, from their handlebars to their wheels.

'You'll get very cold bottoms,' warned Sapphire, clambering on to her bicycle, 'but we'll go really fast. The wheels slide across the frozen Lake without slipping, you see.'

Jessica had also persuaded the craftsman to carve two pairs of special ice skates for Sinbad, who of course could not ride a bicycle.

'Wow!' yelled the donkey, his hooves skidding about as he slid and slithered after the Icicle Bicycles.

Olympia clung to Sinbad's head for dear life. 'Wait for us!' she squawked.

It was great fun to whizz along the frozen Lake on the bicycles, and the cycling made the girls warm up fast.

'But my bottom is freezing!' gasped Valentina.

'Don't worry, we're nearly there.' Sapphire pointed through the mist.

Sure enough, a village was coming into view. There were several more of the little timber houses clustered at the bottom of the tallest Frosty Mountain the girls had ever seen.

'Crys's house is that one, right by the water,' Sapphire said, pointing at a house with a big front yard and a snow-coated wooden fence. 'It's quite a simple place,' she added, glancing at Valentina as they all slithered off the Lake and began to cycle towards the house. 'But simple is good enough for us Lake Dwellers.'

'It's lovely,' said Valentina, who would have agreed to live forever in a tumbledown shack if it had a warm fire and a soft chair to park her frozen behind.

'I'll wait here,' said Sapphire, hanging back as the others went through the gate. 'This is private between you and Crys.'

They leaned their bicycles against the wooden fence and Jessica helped

Sinbad off with his ice skates.

'Do you think there'll be something nice for lunch?' the donkey asked. 'I hear Lake Dwellers eat these things called Vanilla Ice Buns. It's a sticky bun, with ice cream in the middle. Can you think of anything more delicious?'

'They also eat a lot of sardine stew,' said Jessica, severely, 'so don't get too excited.'

'I c-c-c-can't believe we're at Eva Snowdrop's house,' whispered Valentina, as Jessica knocked on the front door.

'Valentina, stop that at once!' Jessica said, sharply. 'That's exactly the reason Crys ran away. If Eva Snowdrop answers the door, you must treat her just like any normal mother, and . . .'

Just then, the front door opened, and a tall, elegant lady looked down at them. 'Yes?' she said.

'Er . . . umm . . . ummph . . . er . . .' was all Jessica could say.

It was Eva Snowdrop.

Although she looked older than in their posters, and although she wore a simple brown tunic rather than a frothy white tutu, Eva was as beautiful as ever. She still held herself like a dancer, with grace and elegance, and the smile she gave Jessica and Valentina was the same smile she had given the audiences at the Palace Theatre many years ago.

'We're here to see C-C-C-Crys,' Valentina found her voice. 'We're her friends from school.'

Eva Snowdrop opened the door wide. 'How nice to meet you! You must all be starving after your long journey. Come into the kitchen, all of you, and you can have a nice hot bowl of leftover sardine stew.'

Sinbad's ears drooped, but he trotted

inside anyway. He was still hoping that he might find a few Vanilla Ice Buns somewhere.

'Crys!' Eva Snowdrop called up the winding staircase as she led them all through to the warm, steamy kitchen. 'There's visitors for you!'

There were hurried footsteps from above and then Crys ran down the stairs, her fox around her shoulders as usual. She went just as white as Pollux when she saw who it was.

'What are you doing here?' she snapped.

Eva Snowdrop gasped. 'Crystal Coldwater, that's no way to speak to your friends. They've come all this way to see you, and in their half-term holiday, too!'

'Half-term holiday?' began Sinbad. 'But it's not a half-term hol–'

Crys turned even more white, fearful that the lie she had told her mother was about to come out. Jessica realised what was going on, and gave Sinbad a small kick.

'It's not a half-term holiday . . . without a fun trip to the Lake!' Sinbad finished.

'Aren't you going to give your friends a hug?' Eva Snowdrop was looking puzzled.

'Friends!' Crys said, in a strange, high voice. 'These aren't my friends. Friends don't betray each others' secrets!'

'Crys, you've got it all wrong . . .' Jessica started to say.

But Crys was not listening. She

pushed past Jessica and Valentina and hurried into the yard. She was just about to run out of the gate when a tall figure blocked her way. It was Sapphire, standing with her hands on her hips.

'Well, well,' she said. 'To think I always thought I was the naughty sister.'

CHAPTER SEVEN
Two Sisters

Crys stared up at her older sister. 'I thought you were meant to be out catching fish for supper.'

'And I thought you were on half-term holiday!' Sapphire's snub nose

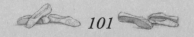

wrinkled and she grinned.

Crys sighed. 'You've met my school-mates, then?'

'Yes,' said Sapphire, 'so now I know it's not half-term at all. Lies have a way of catching up with you.'

'I didn't lie! I just . . . didn't tell the whole truth.' Crys hung her head.

'I know what happened at school,' Sapphire finally said, in a much softer voice than usual. 'Your friends told me.'

'Some friends!' snapped Crys. 'They

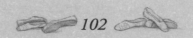

were the ones who couldn't keep their mouths shut.'

'You think they told everyone about Mum?' Sapphire asked. 'Well, maybe if you'd stuck around for a bit longer, instead of running away, you'd have found it was someone else.'

Crys stared at her. 'Who?'

'A girl called "nasty-stinky-Rubellina", or something,' said Sapphire. 'Sounds like a proper madam, she does.'

Crys's mouth fell open. 'Rubellina?'

She felt Pollux's tail perk up. 'So it wasn't my friends!'

'Maybe now you can stop pretending you're on half-term,' Sapphire said, briskly, 'and go straight back to school.'

Crys felt so happy for a moment that she was ready to set off back to Silverberg without a moment's delay. But then she remembered.

'Everything's gone wrong, though, Sapph. School just won't be the same now that everyone knows about Mum.'

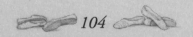

'Whatever are you talking about?' Sapphire demanded.

'It's the same as what happened to you,' Crys muttered. 'Once all your classmates found out, you had to leave.'

'Oh, Crys! Do you think that's why I left the Royal Ballet School?' Sapphire began to chuckle.

'It's not funny!' Crys snapped. Sometimes, she thought, older sisters could be a real pain. 'I loved it there! I've made wonderful friends, and I was doing really well in ballet class, and . . .'

Sapphire and Castor, her fox, both rolled their eyes. 'Well, of course you're doing really well at ballet class, Crys,' said Sapphire. 'You're a brilliant dancer. I wasn't.'

'What?' said Crys.

'It's true,' said Castor. 'She was pretty rotten.'

Sapphire pulled her fox's tail. 'I think I only got in because they knew who

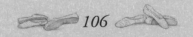

Mum was, and they thought I'd have to get better one day. Well, I didn't. I just got worse and worse. Hated every minute of it, too. That's why I left. I just wasn't cut out to be a dancer.'

Crys could not say a word.

'But you, Crys – well, you could even be as good as Mum one day,' Sapphire continued. 'As long as you go back to school, that is. And work very hard.'

'And don't let a little thing like a bit of silly gossip upset you,' added Castor.

Crys threw her arms around her sister. 'Oh, Sapphire, thank you!'

'Don't thank me,' said Sapphire.

'Thank your friends. They came all this way to get you.'

Crys ran back into the cottage. Jessica, Valentina, Sinbad and Olympia were sitting around the kitchen table. They were not eating leftover sardine stew, but tucking into freshly made Vanilla Ice Buns. Sinbad looked nearly as happy as Crys did.

'Thank you, thank you!' Crys hugged each of her friends in turn, then her mother. 'Everything's all right. I'm the luckiest girl in the whole Kingdom, and I'm going back to school!'

CHAPTER EIGHT
Back to School

Faster than ever now that they had got the hang of their Icicle Bicycles, the little party set off back to Silverberg. Eva Snowdrop packed a bag with Vanilla Ice Buns for the journey, which

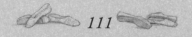

Sinbad promised to keep very safe around his neck.

The way back to Silverberg was simply to follow the setting sun to the south, and soon the city itself came into view across the Drosselmeyer Plains. It was then that the girls began to feel nervous.

'What if we've been found out?' Crys clutched the icy handlebars of the bicycle that Sapphire had given her. Now that they were leaving the freezing North, the bicycles were beginning to melt a little, and she hoped they would make it back to the city before they simply fell into puddles of very cold water. 'It'll all be my fault.'

'Don't worry, Crys. We're all in this together,' said Jessica.

The Icicle Bicycles lasted just until the North Gate, and then the girls continued to make their way along the dark streets on foot.

'We'll need to bribe one of the guards to let us in,' whispered Jessica, as they approached the Palace. 'Sinbad, where are those Vanilla Ice Buns you were keeping safe?'

A guilty expression crossed Sinbad's face. 'Well, they're very safe.'

Jessica glared at him. 'Very safe where, Sinbad?'

'Very safe . . . in my tummy,' admitted Sinbad.

'Sinbad!'

'Hang on, Jess. We may not need to bribe the guards after all,' Crys

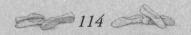

whispered, pointing to where light was coming out of a large window. 'That's the library. Somebody must still be in there.' She picked up a handful of light pebbles from one of the flowerbeds. 'This ought to get their attention.'

'Crys, no!' gasped Valentina. 'What if it's Rubellina?'

But it was too late. Crys had already thrown her handful of pebbles towards the window. They clattered on the glass, and then, as the three girls held their breath, the window opened . . . and two very familiar heads peered out.

'Hello?' said one of the heads.

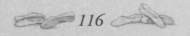

'It's Laura-Bella and Ursula!' squawked Olympia.

Laura-Bella and Ursula helped them all through the window into the empty library. This took several minutes and a great deal of hard work, as Sinbad got stuck, and eventually had to be pulled through by his ears.

'We're so glad you're back!' Laura-Bella flung her arms around Crys. 'You can't imagine the hard day we've had, making sure nobody knew you were gone! Rubellina guessed when you weren't at dinner.'

'She knew Sinbad would never miss dinner,' Ursula added.

'She's bound to have told a teacher, and . . .' Laura-Bella stopped. All of them could hear the same thing.

Footsteps were coming down the passageway outside, towards the library.

'Quick!' Jessica thought fast. 'Everyone, sit at the table and pretend we're working on our project!'

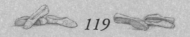

Just as they all scrambled into seats around the nearest table, opening books and seizing pencils, the library door opened. It was Rubellina Goodfellow and, just behind her, Master Silas.

'So you see, Master Silas,' Rubellina was saying, 'I thought I really ought to report them missing. I'm so worried about them, you see . . .'

Now it was her turn to stop short.

'What are you doing here?' Rubellina screeched, staring at the group

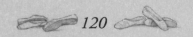

around the table.

'Just working on our project,' Crys said, glancing up from her books. 'Good

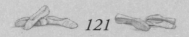

evening, Master Silas.'

Master Silas looked rather crossly down at Rubellina. 'You silly girl, wasting my time! Off to bed with you, before you get into any more mischief!'

Red-faced and pouting, Rubellina skulked away.

'I am glad to see such hard work,' said Master Silas, turning to leave. 'I look forward to reading your project tomorrow. I'm sure it will be one of the very best.' The door closed behind him.

'But we don't even have a project,' said Laura-Bella, in despair, as soon as she knew Master Silas was gone. 'We haven't written anything at all. We've been too busy making sure no one knew you were gone!'

'Even if we sit up all night, we'll never have it done in time,' groaned Ursula, staring at all the dozens of books about Eva Snowdrop that were spread out on the desks. 'Look at all these books we have to read!'

But Crys, Jessica and Valentina smiled.

'We don't need to read about Eva Snowdrop,' said Jessica. 'We just met her!'

'And I can tell you everything you need to know,' said Crys, proudly. 'She's my mum, after all.'

THE END

POLLUX THE FOX'S RECIPE FOR
Vanilla Ice Buns

INGREDIENTS (MAKES 12):

* 3 large cups of fresh Frosty Mountain Snow;
* 1 half-cup of Lake ice, crunched;
* 2 cups of sweet cream, fluffed;
* 1 cup of Vanilla-scented Sugar, for dusting;
* 12 freshly-baked Flaky Vanilla Puff-Buns, according to your family recipe;
* and as many Snowberries as you can pick without your hands freezing.

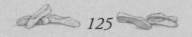

METHOD:

Once you have crunched the Lake ice with your pocket ice-breaker and fluffed the sweet cream with your high-speed cream-fluffer, you are ready to begin. Get your Ice-Bun machine out of the kitchen cupboard, and switch it on. Slowly pour in the fluffed cream and add the fresh snow, taking care that the mixture doesn't get any colder than minus 5 degrees (all good Ice-Bun machines will keep the temperature constant).

Next, get a kitchen chair and your tallest relative, and instruct them to drop handfuls of Snowberries into the mixture from as high up as they possibly can – remember, the louder the splat, the sweeter the ice cream. Once the Snowberries have been splatted to your satisfaction, and the mixture is swirled pink-and-white, add the crunched Lake ice one spoon at a time, until the ice cream is dotted with crunchy crystals.

Now, switch your Ice-Bun machine into Scoop mode, and programme it to make twelve evenly sized ice-cream balls. Take your fresh Puff-Buns, and stuff each one with a ball of ice cream. If your Bun Machine has a Dust mode (newer machines should have this feature), put each Bun through the machine to be dusted with Vanilla-scented Sugar – if not, you will have to do this by hand.

Serve the Buns at once, if possible,

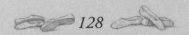

or put them on the outside window sill for later, if you must. But be careful if the weather is very cold outside, or your beautiful Buns will turn into Tooth-Torturing Rock-Ices, which are quite a different matter.

Once you have learnt the basic Vanilla Ice Bun recipe, why not try some tasty variations? White Chocolate ice cream is a delicious alternative filling, and you can dust the Buns with pretty pink Snowberry-Scented Sugar

to make sure you still get that all-important pink-and-white effect. Or, for very special occasions, make one giant Vanilla Ice Bun (set your machine to Giant setting, and shoo away any hungry donkeys that happen to be lurking around your kitchen) and serve it drizzled with sticky Raspberry Syrup and topped with Iced White Chocolate Drops, if you can afford them.

Glossary

Cinnamon Twists: *Long, thin doughnuts that are twisted into a double knot before being freshly fried and then sprinkled with cinnamon sugar. A speciality of Silverberg. Donkeys love them.*

Crocodils and Daffodaisies: Crocodils are yellow or purple wild flowers that grow in spring all over the Kingdom. In fact, wild flowers is a good description – like the crocodiles they sound like, the flowers will give you a little nip on the hand if you try to pick them before they are ready. Daffodaisies are less dangerous. They are tall white-and-yellow daisies the size of daffodils, and perfect for making into long Daffodaisy chains.

Frosting-Stones: Precious stones mined from the Frosty Mountains themselves. They come in several colours — red, green, blue and a deep amber — but the most prized of all are the colourless stones, more beautiful even than our own diamonds. The stones come out of the mountain just as they are, with no need for cutting or polishing. Finding a particularly large Frosting-Stone could make your fortune, but mining them is dangerous and difficult work.

Hot Buttered Flumpets: These are a little bit like the crumpets you eat for tea, but they taste softer and slightly sweeter, and they are shaped like fingers. They are always served piping hot, with melted butter oozing through the holes.

Ice Buns: Made for special occasions in the Lakes, these buns look plain on the outside but are filled with creamy pink-and-white ice cream on the inside. Be careful when you bite in!

Iced White Chocolate Drops: An expensive treat that only the very rich can afford. These chocolate drops are found by divers inside seashells at the very bottom of the northern Lake. They stay ice-cold right up until they are popped into your mouth, where they slowly melt.

Icicle Bicycles: Quite simply, bicycles carved from blocks of ice. They are the best way to travel from one side of the

frozen Lake to the other, as the icy wheels speed you across without any danger of skidding or slipping. But be warned, and pack a cushion — or the icy seat will leave your bottom extremely cold.

Lemon Fizzicles: Lemon-flavoured chewy sweets that fizz with tiny bubbles when you suck them.

Raspberry Flancakes: Flancakes are yeasty, flaky pancakes that rise up to five

or ten centimetres thick when you cook them in a special Flancake pan. Their outside is brown and rich with butter, their inside light and airy. Flancakes can be made in any flavour, but raspberry is the most popular. Donkeys love them, too.

Scoffins: Halfway between a scone and a muffin. They are best served fresh from the oven, split in two, and spread with Snowberry Jam.

Snowberries: Round, plump, juicy berries that grow in hedgerows all over the Kingdom throughout the winter. The snowberries from the south and the west are very dark pink, while the ones that grow in the east and the north are red in colour. Snowberries are always eaten cooked – in jams, Flancakes, waffles or muffins – where they taste sweet but tart at the same time. Don't make the mistake of eating one straight from the hedgerow, however tasty it looks. Uncooked

Snowberries are delicious, but they pop open in your mouth and fill it with a juice so sticky that your teeth are instantly glued together. This can take a whole morning to wear off.

SpringSprung Day: The official first day of spring, and a big day for the inhabitants of the Kingdom after a long, cold winter. SpringSprung Day is marked with a big festival in Silverberg, but the Valley Dwellers throw parties in

139

their own homes for those who would rather not travel the long way to the City. For many, the highlight of the festivities is the SpringSprung Pudding (see below), though many delicious delicacies are served, including lemon-and-orangeade.

SpringSprung Pudding: A sponge pudding, filled with plump currants and chewy dried Snowberries, this is steamed in a huge pudding basin and served in thick slices, sprinkled with sugar, on

SpringSprung Day. One pudding will normally feed ten hungry people. Sinbad can eat a whole pudding all by himself, with room for afters.

Toffee Apple Torte: The speciality of the Grand Café and Tea-Rooms in Silverberg. This tart is made with delicate slices of the fruits that grow in the toffee-apple orchards in the deep south of the Valley, then served warm with toffee-butter sauce.

Who's Who in the Kingdom of the Frosty Mountains

The girls and their pets

Jessica Juniper – *Ballerina from the western Rocks*

Sinbad – *Jessica's pet donkey*

Crystal Coldwater –
Ballerina from the northern Lake

Pollux – *Crystal's pet white fox*

Laura-Bella Bergamotta –
Ballerina from the southern Valley

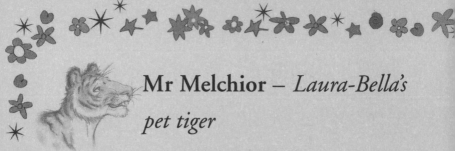

Mr Melchior – *Laura-Bella's pet tiger*

Ursula of the Boughs – *Ballerina from the eastern Forest*

Dorothea – *Ursula's pet bear*

Valentina de la Frou – *Ballerina from the City*

144

Olympia – *Valentina's pet eagle*

Some other Ballerinas

Rubellina Goodfellow – *Ballerina from the City, and the Chancellor's daughter*

Jo-Jo Marshall – *Another Ballerina from the City, and Rubellina's best friend*

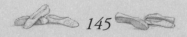

The Teachers

Mistress Odette – *the Headmistress*

Mistress Camomile – *a Ballet teacher*

Master Lysander – *another Ballet teacher, also known as Mustard Stockings*

Master Silas – *the History of Ballet teacher*

Mistress Hawthorne – *the Gym teacher*

Mistress Babette – *the Costume, Hair and Make-up teacher*

Master Jacques – *the Mime teacher*

The Royal Party

King Caspar – *the King*

Queen Mab – *the Queen*

Chancellor Godwin Goodfellow – *the Kingdom's Chancellor*

EGMONT PRESS: ETHICAL PUBLISHING

Egmont Press is about turning writers into successful authors and children into passionate readers – producing books that enrich and entertain. As a responsible children's publisher, we go even further, considering the world in which our consumers are growing up.

Safety First
Naturally, all of our books meet legal safety requirements. But we go further than this; every book with play value is tested to the highest standards – if it fails, it's back to the drawing-board.

Made Fairly
We are working to ensure that the workers involved in our supply chain – the people that make our books – are treated with fairness and respect.

Responsible Forestry
We are committed to ensuring all our papers come from environmentally and socially responsible forest sources.

For more information, please visit our website at
www.egmont.co.uk/ethicalpublishing